The Secret Goldfish

PRAISE FOR *STORYSHARES*

"One of the brightest innovators and game-changers in the education industry."
– Forbes

"Your success in applying research-validated practices to promote literacy serves as a valuable model for other organizations seeking to create evidence-based literacy programs."

- Library of Congress

"We need powerful social and educational innovation, and Storyshares is breaking new ground. The organization addresses critical problems facing our students and teachers. I am excited about the strategies it brings to the collective work of making sure every student has an equal chance in life."
– Teach For America

"Around the world, this is one of the up-and-coming trailblazers changing the landscape of literacy and education."
- International Literacy Association

"It's the perfect idea. There's really nothing like this. I mean wow, this will be a wonderful experience for young people."   - Andrea Davis Pinkney, Executive Director, Scholastic

"Reading for meaning opens opportunities for a lifetime of learning. Providing emerging readers with engaging texts that are designed to offer both challenges and support for each individual will improve their lives for years to come. Storyshares is a wonderful start."
- David Rose, Co-founder of CAST & UDL

The Secret Goldfish

Ariel Morrison

STORYSHARES

Story Share, Inc.
New York. Boston. Philadelphia

Storyshares
Story Share, Inc.
24 N. Bryn Mawr Avenue #340
Bryn Mawr, PA 19010-3304
www.storyshares.org

Inspiring reading with a new kind of book.

Interest Level: Middle School
Grade Level Equivalent: 4.8

9781642612066

Book design by Storyshares

Printed in the United States of America

Storyshares Presents

1

Papa was a hero.

Everyone told me so. I remember when he was standing at the door and hugging Mama good-bye. I didn't know why she was crying; Papa was going to fight the bad guys because he's good, and that's what good guys do. Everyone knows that, even cartoons do. I wanted to tell her not to cry because Papa was a hero like Superman, and Superman was strong and couldn't get hurt by anything.

Papa had kneeled down and hugged me too, and I didn't cry because I was a big boy. Mama said so. Big boys don't cry, so I didn't. But why was Papa crying? He's a man; that's what bigger boys turn into, men. The biggest boys turn into Superman, but that's a very hard level to reach. That's why I said Papa was like Superman because he was on his way there. I asked him too, why he was crying. He smiled and said it was because he loved me and Mama so much. I didn't know a person could be so full of love that they would start crying because how could feelings get to be that big? Maybe when people grow bigger, their feelings grow bigger too, but that didn't make sense to me because Mama and Papa were bigger than me, and I wasn't crying at all.

He said he was proud of me and to keep doing well in school. I already knew that; he didn't have to tell me. But he did tell me something very important, and I made sure to stick to it.

2

      I don't know how long it's been since Papa left. I think it's been a year because I have all his letters. I'm looking at them right now, you know. The first one is from February 1942, and he talks about how he's in Britain training for something big, but he doesn't know what that something is. No one does. I thought that was cool because it was just like in comic books where only the powerful guys know what's going on, like the big-shot generals or something, maybe even the president. When the big guys know something no one else knows, you know it's something super important.

I showed the letter to Mama when it came, and she practically ripped open the envelope trying to get to the letter. That annoyed me a little because envelopes are just as important as letters; they keep the words from falling out. I wanted to save it, but I knew how eager Mama was, so I didn't say anything. She hugged the letter to her chest and smiled, like she could feel Papa hugging her back through the paper. It was like this every time we got a letter, but when I told her I wanted to save the envelopes, she opened them much more carefully. I thought about making a scrapbook and showing it to Papa when he came home, but I wasn't good at stuff like that.

Anyways, when that first letter came, Mama sat down and wrote back a super long letter, and I did the same. Hers was pretty and organized, like a letter should be. I wanted my letter to be just as nice as Mama's, but my cursive wasn't as good as hers. I made a comic strip instead, because I was pretty sure you couldn't have comic books in the army, and Papa would probably be dying for something to read. He was a big reader, you know. Maybe his job in the army was to read stuff, like maps or codes or something. I never got to ask him that.

3

In school we talked a lot about the war. We listened to the radio a lot more, and we started learning about different countries and how some were good and some were bad. Mrs. Clark showed us how this country called Japan bombed Pearl Harbor, all the way out in Hawaii. We looked at before and after pictures of Pearl Harbor, and it scared me how strong Japan was. Mrs. Clark said that we would defeat Japan because our country was much more advanced than they were, but I wasn't sure about that.

They were strong enough to hurt one of our bases, and we didn't catch what they were up to until our harbor was bombed.

I don't know. I really don't. I guess it's one of those things you don't know how to describe. I mean, you wouldn't know how to describe feeling scared for no reason without sounding like you're crazy. But I got scared. Scared because of what the Japanese did, but it made me respect them a little too. They grew so strong in just a short amount of time, and I thought that we could learn from how well they adapted to their surroundings. That was something most people couldn't do, but a whole country did it, and I didn't know if I could hate something but still have respect for it, especially when Papa was supposed to be fighting them.

I raised my hand and told Mrs. Clark what I thought about Japan, and she gave me a scary look and told me to see her after school.

What I learned in class was that you gotta know when to keep your mouth shut.

4

Train tracks are great. They really are. They're one of the greatest things in the world, and I'm not lying. I have history to prove it. If you could sit next to me on the tracks right now and feel what I'm feeling, you'd know. Don't tell anyone I ever come here though; Mama said that it's dangerous to sit on a track, but I don't know why. You could hear a train coming from miles away, and you'd have plenty of time to hop off and hide somewhere and watch the train roll by. Only the front of the train is loud because that's where the engine is. All the train cars following it are pretty silent, and most people are pretty surprised to learn that.

I like watching the trains go by. They're really long and could go on forever, and they're so colorful. Sometimes you see graffiti on the train cars, and that makes me happy. Even though some of it is pretty ugly, it still makes me happy because that meant that someone wanted to leave their mark somewhere, so everyone could see it. People forget that other people are alive too, and stuff like graffiti makes you remember you're not the only person who exists.

Usually the place I go to watch the train is empty; there's just a bunch of cardboard boxes and old tires and junk people throw away. You wouldn't believe the stuff people throw away sometimes. Today I found a burnt-out TV set, and I messed around with the buttons for a bit. I liked turning the knob the most, though. I turned and turned it and listened to the clicking noise it made every time it passed a number. That stuff can't keep you entertained forever, though; what makes it interesting is the fact that you can't do things like that often. When you have too much of it, it becomes normal just like everything else.

Something shone in the dirt, and I bent down behind a flap of cardboard to dig it up. At first I thought it was a dime or something, and I got excited because I started thinking about what comic book I could buy with it. It was just a piece of aluminum, but I used it to doodle in the dirt for a while. Then I heard something crunch, and I froze. I hoped it wasn't the police or anything because they'd bring me home to Mama, and I'd have to tell her where I was. I held my breath and peeked over the cardboard.

5

Oh. It was just a kid. He looked the same age as me, and he was muttering to himself as he picked at the trash.

"Hey," I came out from behind the cardboard and waved the aluminum at him. He froze where he was, and I started walking towards him. "Hey." I never saw a kid run as fast as he did. I chased him down the track and threw the aluminum stick off somewhere. "I just wanted to say hi!"

Then he tripped over a rock and tumbled down pretty bad, and he started crying. "Don't tell on me, please," he sobbed. "Please don't, don't tell." He looked up at me, bawling like crazy.

"Why would I tell? I come down here all the time too. I like your hair, it's really neat." I sat down next to him, catching my breath. He scooted away from me, but I didn't scoot closer. It's important to respect personal space. "How's your leg? Is it bleeding?"

He was still crying but a lot more quietly. He shifted his arm so it covered his leg up, but I could still see where it was scraped up. It was pretty bad. "M-my leg is fine. Go away."

"I can see it bleeding though. I could help if you want. I'm Alfred. I won't tell on you, I swear. There's nothing *to* tell anyways." I pulled out the handkerchief Mama always made me carry. I always thought it was stupid, but for once I was glad that I had it with me. "Here, use this. You can use it to clean up your leg, and I'll just tell my mom that I spilled Kool-Aid on it or something."

He peered at me suspiciously, then slowly took the handkerchief and dabbed at his leg with it silently.

"What's your name? You look a lot different than everyone else I know." He froze up at that. "That's okay though." I continued. "It'd be boring if *every*one was the same." Then he relaxed.

"I'm Kiku."

"Kee-koo." I repeated. "That's cool. Can I call you Keeks?"

He finished wiping the dirt and blood off his scrapes and nodded. "Thank you for letting me use your handkerchief, Alfred." He folded it meticulously and handed it back to me. I took it and stuffed it back in my pocket.

"Yea, sure. That's what people are supposed to do. Hey, why were you crying so much earlier?" We started walking side by side next to the train tracks, back towards the way we came.

He glanced at me. "You don't know?"

I shrugged. "There's lots of things I don't know, Keeks."

Kiku nodded. "I'm Japanese." He said quickly, like he just wanted to push out the words and leave them in front of me. I stared at him, my mouth hanging open slightly. I had never met a Japanese person before. In school everyone said Japanese people were ugly and bad. There were even posters of buck-toothed yellow people in white uniforms in the hallways and on buildings, but they were just drawings. Drawings of people in posters almost never looked like people in real life.

"How come you're not yellow?" He looked down, and I could tell I hurt his feelings. I didn't mean to. I was honestly curious why those posters showed Japanese people as yellow when Kiku was right here in front of me and was whiter than me. "I'm sorry, I really am."

"It's okay, I understand." Kiku said quietly. We had reached the place where I first saw him. He stopped and turned to me. "You really won't tell anyone?"

I groaned. "Keeks, if I really was going to tell, I would've known you were Japanese when I first saw you." I pointed out.

He nodded again. "I just want to be sure. There's no one to trust anymore, Alfred."

6

"Why? You live here, don't you?" I asked.

Kiku looked around nervously and then leaned in close to me. "I *do* live here. But I'm Japanese, and since we're fighting against Japan, the government thinks that we'll spy on them or something. So they're moving us out of our houses. They're putting us in camps, Alfred." He glanced at me sadly. "I don't even know that much Japanese. I was born *here*."

I didn't know what to say. We were supposed to be the good guys. Only bad guys took people away from their homes. I suddenly grasped Kiku's pinky with mine and squeezed it. "I won't tell anyone, Kiku. I pinky promise."

He seemed startled at first, then gave me a small smile and squeezed back with his pinky. "Stay here." Kiku ran off and disappeared behind a dirty white fence. I stared at the fence he went behind for a while, then walked towards the train tracks and sat there, waiting some more. I almost thought he changed his mind and was standing up to leave when he reappeared, carrying a baggie with him.

"Sorry I took a long time. I wanted to give you this." He thrust the bag at me, and I stared at it. The bag was filled with water, and a goldfish was swimming inside, staring at me. I shook my head.

"You don't have to give it to me, really."

"No, take it Alfred. My mom told me that in Japan, it means peace."

I stared back at the fish and fisted my hand in my pocket, wishing I had something to give back to Kiku. My fingers brushed across something, and I pulled it out: a nickel. I think I was saving it up for something, but I couldn't remember what. I held it out to Kiku. "Then you take this. I get a fish; you get a nickel. We both get something."

Kiku stared at me, then held out his palm. We swapped quickly, and I folded my hardkerchief around the bag and stuffed it under my jacket. We stood quietly for a bit, then waved at each other and ran off. He went back to the fence, and I ran down the dirt road that I took to the tracks.

I told you train tracks are great.

7

When I was finally home, I gave Mama a quick kiss on the cheek and beat it to my room. I tried not to slam the door, but it still slammed anyways. That happens when I get too eager. I put the baggie on my bed and changed into my pajamas, then stared at the goldfish. It looked pretty neat. I never thought that animals and fish and reptiles could mean something, but I guess everything means something when you think about it.

It made me sad when I thought how the goldfish meant peace and how I got my first pet from a Japanese kid. I don't mean it made me sad in a bad way because I really did like the goldfish. I meant how a Japanese kid who didn't really know that much about Japan gave me a fish that meant peace, and how Mrs. Clark was telling us that Japan was bad and didn't know anything about peace, and how my papa left because he was fighting against the bad guys, and *Japan* was one of the bad guys. Nothing made sense anymore. I thought that good and bad were so easy to tell apart. If Japan was bad, that meant Kiku was bad because he was Japanese. But he said that we were moving them out of his home and putting them in weird camps, so that would make us the bad guys, and if we were the bad guys, then that meant that Papa was a bad guy too. But Kiku seemed like one of the nicest people I knew, and Papa would never do anything bad.

My door opened, and I shoved the goldfish under my pillow. That didn't seem like the best place to put it because if the bag broke, my bed would get wet, and my goldfish would be squished to death.

"Hey honey," Mama said and sat next to me on my bed.

"Hi Mama," I said back, confused. Mama usually never came into my room unless it was dirty or if I did something bad. My room was pretty clean right now though, and I couldn't remember doing anything bad.

She kissed my forehead and brushed my hair back, and then she hugged me. We hugged for a very long time, and my arms were getting tired, but I didn't want to push Mama away. Then she let go of me and kissed my cheek. "I love you, Alfred. You know that, don't you?"

"Yea, I love you too, Mama." I said back to her and looked at her to see what was wrong. She kissed my cheek again and then left my room.

I closed the door behind her, wishing I hadn't looked at Mama. I pulled my goldfish out from under my pillow and tried hugging the baggie without squeezing it too much.

Mama was crying.

The Secret Goldfish

8

I didn't go to recess at school. I went to the library instead, which made the librarian look at me like I was crazy because recess is my favorite part of the day. I really needed to find out how to take care of goldfish, though. I remembered that I never asked Kiku what goldfish even ate, or how many times they eat in a day, or even if I should take the goldfish out of the bag. I bet it was getting real tired of being stuck inside that tiny bag.

I asked Mrs. Thrower, the librarian, where the books on goldfish were. She gave me the old eyeball, wondering what I was up to, because the last time I was in here I tried doing an experiment on an apple. Mrs. Thrower pointed down to the Nature for Kids aisle, and I followed her finger until I found a book on goldfish. I opened it up to the part where it said, "Diet and Habitat," and skipped all the boring parts.

Although goldfish love plant material and algae, they do require the mix of animal protein and plant protein to really thrive, the book said. I didn't know fish needed protein. *Peas are a great supplement to your goldfish's diet.* That was cool. I hated peas. I kept reading and found that goldfish really liked white rice and broccoli. I wasn't sure if my goldfish would be able to survive on just that, but it was better than asking Mama for money to feed an imaginary goldfish.

How many times did I need to change the water though? I read through the book again: *every seven to ten days.* Dang. I didn't know where I would dump all the old water out. Down the sink maybe, but it would be hard running down the hall hiding a goldfish every week. I didn't want to keep the goldfish in a bag, though. Then it hit me. I could just keep the goldfish in a giant Dixie cup! If I put it on my shelf with my books and made sure nothing would fall on it, it would be just right. Then I wouldn't have to keep opening and reopening the bag to feed the goldfish, and when I had to change the water, I would look like I was walking to get water for myself.

I smiled. My fish would be fine.

9

I wondered when I would see Kiku again. It had been two weeks since I met him, and I wondered if he was thinking the same thing about me. I really wanted to tell him how good the goldfish was doing, but I hadn't named it yet. It just seemed right to me that he should name it because he didn't have to give it to me. That was why I gave him a nickel, so I would at least feel like I bought it.

I went back to the tracks on the weekend, and the burnt-out TV and tires and old cardboard were still there, so I sat down next to the cardboard flap again and waited. I found a stick and drew in the dirt again, and I wondered if Kiku knew I was out here or if he was hiding because he didn't want to be sent to the camps. I should've asked him if we could meet up again. He was a pretty cool person.

A train passed by, announcing its arrival with a rumble and honked its horn as it passed by me. I waved to the conductor, and I stared at the graffiti plastered on the train cars, and I wondered if Kiku looked at the graffiti too and what he thought about it. I wondered if he even liked trains at all or if he was too scared to come out to look at the train because of someone possibly seeing him.

I waited until the sun set, and I threw down the stick and kicked the dirt up as I walked home.

10

It had been months since Papa's last letter came. The last one was from July 1942.

It was 1943 now.

I wasn't sure what to think. Maybe Papa was in such a top-secret mission that he had to change his identity to protect us and couldn't write to us because his cover might be blown. Maybe his letters got lost in the mail somewhere. Maybe he can't send mail because it might be taken by the bad guys. I didn't want to think of the other realistic options.

Mama tried to act all calm about it, but I could tell she was worried. She was worried sick and frantic about Papa, and she kept herself busy by constantly cleaning the house and shopping for groceries and buying me new clothes. I asked her if we could get a colorful vase so I could put it in my room to give it more color, and she bought it without even questioning me, which was weird because I've never cared much about colors anyways. I felt bad for taking advantage of her, but I figured out that I couldn't keep my goldfish in a paper cup forever. It deserved more than that.

Then the day came when Papa came home. There was a knock at the door, and Mama rushed to open it. A man in a brown army dress uniform stood on the porch, tall and mighty. I didn't remember Papa being so tall like that. I didn't know adults could still grow.

Mama didn't remember Papa being that tall either because she just stared at the man. "Brandon?" She whispered.

The man saluted. "Mrs. Jones, I am Officer Perryman." He handed Mama a square envelope. "I am proud to say that your husband lived nobly and died honorably in the service of the United States military," he said gently. Mama looked at him in horror, unwilling to accept the letter. I walked forward and took it for her, and Officer Perryman glanced down at me sympathetically. "Your father was a great man. I served alongside him in Italy with the 1-186th Battalion."

"Thank you," I said quietly. Officer Perryman nodded, walked down the porch and into a black car, and drove away. I closed the door, and Mama sank down to the floor and wailed miserably. I cried silently.

I forgot that Superman wasn't invincible.

11

I stared at my goldfish. It swam around in the vase like it always did, but it looked like it was trying extra hard to breathe. I couldn't remember the last time I changed its water. I had been too empty to really think about anything else, and suddenly I felt bad for just forgetting about the goldfish like that.

I picked up the vase and peeked out of my room, making sure that Mama couldn't see me. She didn't pay that much attention to me now. Don't get me wrong,

Mama still took care of me and hugged me and everything, but I guess she was taking it harder than me. I rushed down to the bathroom and put the goldfish in a Dixie cup full of water. Then I ran outside to the back and dumped the water on Mama's plants. Her flowers were dying, and I was practically the only reason they ever got watered anymore.

When I got back, the goldfish was just sitting in the water. I panicked and thought it was dead, but when I nudged it with my finger it moved around again but really slow. I thought maybe I hadn't fed it because I couldn't remember when it last ate, either. So after I put the fish back in the vase, I opened up the frozen bag of peas from the freezer and took a handful, then ran back to my room and dumped them in the vase.

I glared at it while it ate, but it didn't care. I was jealous how the goldfish could lead such a simple life. Literally all it did was eat and poop and swim. If I could trade places with a goldfish, would I? I seriously thought about that for a while, but I decided that I wouldn't. I wouldn't trade places with the goldfish even if things were at their worst. I wondered if Kiku would though. I didn't know if goldfish meant anything in America, but Kiku told me they meant a lot in Japan, how they represented peace and everything.

Maybe he wouldn't, either. It would suck being a goldfish, just swimming around and eating and pooping whenever you felt like it. I mean, I guess if you like the *simple* parts of life it would be nice, but you wouldn't really be able to feel anything that mattered.

I don't understand life.

I don't think you're supposed to.

The Secret Goldfish

12

It was sunny when we had Papa's funeral.

I didn't know if I should've been happy or sad or mad about that. I didn't like the idea that everyone else could be so happy and that some people could be at Disneyland with their dads and other people could be playing baseball or just laying down in the grass enjoying the sun. I wanted everyone to feel as sad as I felt today.

But at the same time, I didn't. I didn't want people knowing how sad I felt or knowing that they wouldn't be able to see someone forever or what it feels like to have a hole in the family.

I didn't want to be here because it didn't feel right having a funeral with an empty box. I hated how the song they played on the bagpipes made me cry, and I hated how the soldiers who folded the flag handed it to my mom with stony faces. They saluted us, and I only saluted back because not saluting would have disrespected Papa. Then seven more soldiers aimed their rifles and, in unison, shot into the air three times.

And for some weird reason, that made me think about Kiku.

13

I took my goldfish back to the train tracks, to the place where I met Kiku. I forgot to feed it, and it died. This time, I took the colorful vase with me, and the water sloshed around in it. I was too depressed to change the water out, and that might've been another reason it was dead.

I stood in between the train tracks and thought about burying the fish there so it could enjoy the trains too, but then I remembered the dirty white fence that

Kiku went back to. It was a tight squeeze. Kiku was skinnier than I thought, but I managed to push myself through without scraping the vase.

It was like travelling to another world. After following a dirt road strewn with trash, I popped into a small dirt clearing, and there were tiny houses made out of scraps of trash, sheet metal, boxes, and scratched up soda bottles. Even though everything was ragged and dusty and mismatched, there was still a strange charm to it; you could smell the dignity and pride here. I could tell how the boxes were carefully set up to resemble tables, how the sheet metal walls were trimmed to fit one another just right, how each hovel still held its own personality.

I suddenly felt ashamed that someone as nice as Kiku was forced to live like this, how we pretended to be the great heroes who swooped in to save everyone when really, we were just as bad as Japan. Maybe there was no such thing as good or bad; people just chose to live with the better option.

I walked into one of the houses when a ray of light bounced into my eyes. I blinked rapidly and squinted at the source. There were shards of broken glass scattered in the dirt, as if someone had thrown it down as hard as they could. In the middle were two fish skeletons, the bones cracked and dry. I looked at my own dead goldfish in the vase, and it floated in the cloudy water pathetically. I scooped it out of the vase and placed it down gently next to the fish skeletons, which I assumed used to be Kiku's. Then I smashed my vase, too. One of the shards ricocheted and cut my finger, but I didn't care. At least the goldfish was back home.

When I slipped out from the fence, it looked dirtier than usual. I guess I didn't pay attention to how much dirt was on it, but then again I don't really pay attention to things like that. I shoved my hands in my jacket and walked down the train tracks and the dirt road. I remembered what Papa said to me before he left: *Don't be afraid to keep secrets, Alfred. Sometimes they're the most valuable things to have.*

I hoped Kiku knew that I kept his secret.

The Secret Goldfish

About The Author

Ariel Morrison was born and raised in the deserts of California. She first started writing when she was twelve years old and often shared her work online in story forums that encouraged its users to read and review stories submitted by others. When she's not writing, she loves to play video games, practice the piano, read historical fiction, and try drawing (even though she's not very good at it). She also loves to travel, and though she has not been outside of the United States yet, she has traveled to sixteen different states. Currently a student at Norwich University, she is working towards earning her degree in Mandarin Chinese as well as a commission in the U.S. Army as a Second Lieutenant.

About The Publisher

Story Shares is a nonprofit focused on supporting the millions of teens and adults who struggle with reading by creating a new shelf in the library specifically for them. The ever-growing collection features content that is compelling and culturally relevant for teens and adults, yet still readable at a range of lower reading levels.

Story Shares generates content by engaging deeply with writers, bringing together a community to create this new kind of book. With more intriguing and approachable stories to choose from, the teens and adults who have fallen behind are improving their skills and beginning to discover the joy of reading. For more information, visit storyshares.org.

Easy to Read. Hard to Put Down.

The Secret Goldfish

www.ingramcontent.com/pod-product-compliance
Lightning Source LLC
Chambersburg PA
CBHW071226170626
46809CB00005BA/1956